Frankie
the Make-up
Fairy

To Aleka with lots of love

Special thanks to
Rachel Elliot

ORCHARD BOOKS
338 Euston Road, London NW1 3BH
Orchard Books Australia
Level 17/207 Kent Street, Sydney, NSW 2000
A Paperback Original

First published in 2012 by Orchard Books

HiT entertainment

Illustrations © Orchard Books 2012

A CIP catalogue record for this book is available
from the British Library.

ISBN 978 1 40831 593 4

3 5 7 9 10 8 6 4

Printed in Great Britain

The paper and board used in this paperback are natural recyclable
products made from wood grown in sustainable forests. The
manufacturing processes conform to the environmental regulations
of the country of origin.

Orchard Books is a division of Hachette Children's Books,
an Hachette UK company

www.hachette.co.uk

Frankie
the Make-up
Fairy

by Daisy Meadows

ORCHARD

www.rainbowmagic.co.uk

Fairyland Music Festival

A-ok trailer

Rehearsal tent

Star Village

Picnic hill

Beach ↗

Jack Frost's Spell

It's high time for the world to see
The legend I was born to be.
The prince of pop, a dazzling star
My fans will flock from near and far.

But pop star fame is hard to get
Unless I help myself, I bet.
I need a plan, a cunning trick
To make my stage act super-slick.

Seven magic clefs I'll steal
They'll give me pop star powers, I feel.
I'll sing and dance, I'll dazzle and shine
And pop star glory will be mine!

Contents

Make-up Mix-up

The sun was shining on best friends Rachel Walker and Kirsty Tate. It was the summer holidays, and they had come to the Rainspell Island Music Festival as special guests of their favourite pop group, The Angels.

The girls were standing among the cluster of activity tents known as Star Village. There were tents of every shape and colour, with fortune-tellers, singing teachers, musicians and stylists offering their services for free. It was hard to know which one to choose!

"Let's try that one," said Rachel.

She pointed to a tent that sparkled in the morning sun. The sign hanging outside said "Glitter & Go", and people were lining up to have their faces painted.

As the girls joined the queue, a group of teenagers walked past, chatting about the famous people they had spotted.

"I heard that Dakota May's here," said one of the boys.

Kirsty and Rachel gasped. Dakota May was one of their favourite pop stars.

"I hope she's going to put on a concert while she's here!" said Kirsty.

They started singing Dakota May's latest song, *The Faces of Me*, and they only stopped when it was their turn to have their faces painted. Giggling, the girls hurried into the tent and perched on high stools.

"Hi, I'm Chloe," said a bubbly dark-haired girl to Rachel. "What would you like today?"

Rachel knew exactly what she wanted!

"Could I have a rainbow across my cheek?" she asked. "Sure thing," said Chloe, picking up her pot of make-up brushes.

"How about you?" asked the red-haired make-up artist in front of Kirsty. "I'm Dora, by the way."

"I can't decide what to have!" said Kirsty with a smile.

"How about some glittery face paint?" asked Dora. "I can make you shimmer like a fairy!"

Rachel and Kirsty shared a smile. No one else knew that they were secretly friends with the fairies. Rainspell Island was a very special place for them, because it was here that they had met the fairies for the first time. Now, as well as enjoying the festival, they were helping the fairies again.

Mean Jack Frost had stolen the Pop Star Fairies' magical musical clefs and brought them to the festival. The clefs made sure that all aspects of pop music were a success, but now Jack Frost was planning to use them to become a pop star himself!

So far, Kirsty and Rachel had helped
four of the Pop Star Fairies to get their
magic clefs back from the goblins who
were hiding them. But there were still
three left to find. Without them, pop
music would be ruined. The girls were
determined not to let that happen.

Just then, a teenage girl with long
blonde hair and large sunglasses sat
down on the stool
next to Kirsty.
"Could
I have a
butterfly on
my cheek,
please?"
she asked.
Her make-up
artist, Sylvie, started work.

The teenager glanced over at Rachel.

"That's going to look very cool," she said. "Maybe *I'll* get a rainbow on my face tomorrow."

"Isn't this a fun festival?" said Rachel, smiling back at her. "We've been trying to decide which bit we like best, but we can't!"

"I know the feeling," said the girl with a friendly laugh. "I've been coming here for years and I still can't decide!"

Rachel and Kirsty chatted to the girl about the other festivals she had attended. She seemed to have been to them all! Meanwhile the make-up artists worked quickly, and when they finished they held up a mirror in front of the girls. Rachel and Kirsty held their breath, ready to be impressed. But...

"Oh," said Kirsty.

"Oh dear," said Rachel.

Kirsty's green and black face paint
made her look more like
a wicked witch
than a fairy.
Rachel's
rainbow
was a messy
blob of dull
colours, and
the blonde
girl had
a spooky spider on her cheek instead of
a beautiful butterfly.

The make-up artists both looked
embarrassed, and Sylvie blushed.

"I can't understand it," said Dora,
frowning at her make-up brushes.

"We have to stop work," said Chloe. "Something weird's going on."

They left the tent and Rachel and Kirsty gazed unhappily at each other. This was all because of Jack Frost and his naughty goblins.

"Don't be sad," said the teenage girl, looking at their glum faces. "Maybe we can fix it."

As she leaned forward to look at the rainbow on Rachel's cheek, her long blonde hair slipped to one side. It was a wig! Underneath the girls caught a glimpse of a black bob, which they recognised at once.

"I know who you are," said Rachel in a thrilled whisper. "You're Dakota May!"

17

Secret Star!

Dakota pulled off her sunglasses and gazed at them pleadingly.

"Please don't say anything," she said. "I'll be mobbed by people wanting autographs, and I just want to chill out at the festival like any normal teenager."

For a moment, Rachel and Kirsty just stared at her in awe. Then a group of boys and girls rushed into the tent, shouting and squealing.

"Is she in here?"

"Has anyone seen her?"

"Where is she?"

"We want Dakota May!"

"Quick, hide!" said Rachel.

She pointed to a full-length mirror in the corner and Dakota darted behind it. Rachel and Kirsty turned to face the excited teenagers.

"Dakota May?" said Rachel in a loud voice. "Did I see her go into the dance tent next door?"

"Or was it the karaoke tent?" Kirsty wondered aloud.

"In any case, I definitely can't see her in here," added Rachel, gazing around.

"Let's go and check out the dance tent!" shouted one of the boys. "Come on!"

The teenagers left the tent and Dakota stepped out from behind the mirror.

"Have they gone?" she asked. "Thanks, girls! It's great that I have so many fans, but sometimes I just want to act like an ordinary girl. Besides, everyone will see me soon – I'm going to be making a surprise appearance at tonight's concert."

Kirsty and Rachel were very excited to hear this news. They had been planning to go to the concert anyway, but now they were determined not to miss it for the world!

"We're really looking forward to it," said Kirsty. "We love your music."

"That's great to hear!" said Dakota with a beaming smile. "I'm

just going for a quiet walk first – hopefully without any fans chasing me!"

"We'll keep your secret," Rachel promised with a grin.

Dakota peered into the mirror and checked that her wig

and sunglasses were on straight.

"Thanks again, girls," she said, heading out of the tent. "Maybe I'll see you at the concert later."

"Definitely!" called Rachel and Kirsty.

As Dakota disappeared from sight, Rachel noticed something strange. A tiny glow was coming from a bundle of make-up brushes on a table.

"Kirsty!" said Rachel in an excited whisper. "Look!"

The glow grew brighter, and then the fattest make-up brush let out a puff of rainbow-coloured fairy dust. Out of the sparkling dust sprang a beautiful fairy! Her dark, pixie-cropped hair gleamed in the light and she giggled as she twirled in midair, shaking the glittering fairy dust from her floaty blue skirt. It was Frankie the Make-up Fairy!

"Hi, girls," she said. "I came to look for my clef, but I was hoping that I'd find you as well!" She frowned. "What's the matter with your face paint?"

The girls quickly explained what had happened. Frankie waved her wand and the horrid designs disappeared from their faces.

"This is bad," she said. "Some of the best make-up artists in the world are here on Rainspell Island. If they can't create beautiful make-up designs, no one can! It's all because my clef is missing."

"That's what we thought," said Kirsty.

"We have to find your necklace fast," said Rachel in a determined voice. "Let's start by looking around Star Village."

Kirsty held open her shoulder bag and Frankie slipped inside. No one must catch a glimpse of the pretty little fairy!

As Rachel and Kirsty left the Glitter & Go tent, they noticed a long queue for the next tent along.

It definitely hadn't been that popular earlier, and it was a very boring-looking tent compared to the others. It was a pale green colour, and it was covered in splashes of mud.

"What's going on here?" Rachel asked a boy who was standing in the queue. "What are you queuing for?"

"It's a face-painting tent," the boy replied. "They're doing the coolest designs ever! I'm going to get a lion on my face!"

Three children were just leaving the tent, and the girls looked at them curiously. Sure enough, they had wonderful designs on their faces – a blue dolphin, a colourful clown and a beautiful princess.

"How did they get such lovely make-up when Frankie's magical clef is missing?" asked Rachel.

"I think we should investigate,"
said Kirsty.

The sign outside the tent was roughly
painted on an old tin tray.

Great Grins by Greeny

They peered into the tent. Inside, a boy
was sitting on a low stool. The make-up
artist who was about to paint his face
was very short, very ugly and very,
very *green*.

"It's a goblin!" Kirsty exclaimed.

"And he's wearing my magical clef
necklace!" cried Frankie.

Goblin Glamour

"I think your face paint is brilliant, Greeny!" the boy was saying. "I want to be a green alien like you! Can you give me a long nose and big feet too? And a necklace just like yours? I want to look exactly the same as you!"

He thought that the goblin's green face was painted on! Greeny muttered something under his breath and wiped his make-up brush on his white tunic.

Suddenly, a plan flashed into Rachel's mind.

"Come around to the back of the tent," she said in a low voice. "I've got an idea."

When they were out of sight, Frankie fluttered out of the bag.

"What's your plan?" she asked eagerly.

"We have to get into the tent," said Rachel. "Frankie, can you turn me into a fairy and make Kirsty look like a pop star? Then she can distract the goblin while I try to get the necklace back."

"Great plan!" said Frankie, her eyes sparkling with mischief.

She waved her wand, and a flurry of tiny golden mirrors flew from the tip and swirled around Rachel. Instantly, she felt herself shrinking to Frankie's size. Pale pink, gauzy wings appeared on her back and she fluttered them in delight. It felt wonderful to be a fairy again!

"Now it's Kirsty's turn!" she said.

Frankie held her wand high above her head and quickly chanted a magic spell.

"To play a game of 'let's pretend',
Please glitz and glam my human friend.
This pop princess will light the sky,
And turn all heads as she walks by."

She flourished her wand in a circle, and a stream of sparkling sequins flowed around Kirsty.

After a few seconds they melted away. Kirsty had been completely transformed into a glamorous pop star!

She was wearing skinny jeans and a
glittering loose top. Super-cool sunglasses
covered her eyes, and her hair was
shaped into a spiky, ultra-modern
style. Twinkling rings
covered her fingers,
and on her arm
was an oversized
sequinned bag.

"You look
brilliant!"
said Rachel,
clapping her
hands together
in delight. "This
will definitely fool
the goblin."

"I feel really tall!" giggled Kirsty,
gazing down at her wedge shoes.

She opened her bag to let Frankie and
Rachel zoom inside. Then she walked
around to the front of the tent. The
children in the queue stared at her in
amazement. She could hear their
curious whispers.

"Who's that girl?"

"She looks so cool!"

"She must be really famous."

At that moment, the boy with the
goblin face paint
came out of
the tent.

"Now's
your chance!"
whispered
Frankie, who
was peeping
out of the bag.

"I can't jump the queue," said Kirsty in a low voice.

Frankie gave a little chuckle.

"You're a pop star," she said. "You can do anything you like!"

Kirsty's heart was thumping hard, but she walked forward with confidence, and the queue parted to let her through. She strode right into the tent and sat  down in front of Greeny the goblin. *Just remember that you're famous*, she told herself. *Be brave!*

Kirsty knew that one of Jack Frost's
goblins would only be impressed by
someone who was proud and rude. She
lifted her chin into the air.

"*I* am the most famous pop star at the
festival," she said in a haughty voice.
"*You* are the best make-up artist here.
So I'm giving you the honour of making
up my face."

Sure enough, Greeny looked thrilled.

"Thank you, Your Starriness... Your Popship... Your Famousness," he stammered. "This is a great honour!"

With trembling hands he opened his make-up box, which was filled with pots of colourful face paint and powdery glitter. Rachel and Frankie peeked out of the sequinned bag and saw Kirsty point to the clef necklace.

"That's a pretty necklace!" she said. "Aren't you afraid that you'll get make-up all over it? I'd take it off if I were you."

"Anything you say!" said Greeny, gazing adoringly at the famous pop star.

Rachel and Frankie squeezed each other's hand in glee. The plan was working perfectly!

39

Rachel in Danger!

"I'll put it somewhere safe," Greeny continued.

The girls hoped that he would put the necklace down on the table, but instead he slipped it into the pocket of his tunic. Rachel flitted out of the bag and hovered behind Greeny.

"Distract him!" she mouthed to Kirsty.

If her best friend could keep him busy, she might be able to take back the necklace without him noticing.

"I want you to tell me all about make-up colours," said Kirsty, looking the goblin straight in the eye. "Which colours should I be wearing?"

"Er ..." said Greeny, looking confused. "You suit ... um... bright colours like... er ... green."

"But what sort of green?" Kirsty demanded.

He just gawped at her with wide eyes. He didn't know what to say.

"Show me the sort of green you mean," she ordered.

"Yes, Your Celebrityness," he babbled. "I'll find some!"

As he hunted through his make-up pots, Rachel quietly slipped into his pocket. It was dark in there, and it smelled of unwashed socks, but she held her breath and felt around for the necklace. As soon as she had the clef in her hands, she zoomed upwards.

But as she flew out of the pocket towards Frankie, there was a loud clap of thunder. With a flash of lightning, someone appeared in the middle of the tent – a person with spiky hair and a very grumpy expression.

"It's Jack Frost!" gasped Frankie in horror. "Quick, Rachel – you must hide!"

Rachel darted into Greeny's make-up kit with the necklace, as Jack Frost marched up to Greeny with his hands on his hips.

"I've been waiting at the Ice Castle for you!" he roared. "What are you doing here, you daft green goblin? I want the magical clef so I can do my make-up! Where is it?"

Greeny reached into his pocket, and his face fell.

"It's g-g-gone!" he stammered.

Jack Frost looked as if he was going to explode with rage. Even the tips of his spiky hair were quivering.

"You've lost my magical clef?" he bellowed. "You blithering idiot!"

Just then, something awful happened. Inside the make-up kit, some of the glittery powder went up Rachel's nose. It prickled and tickled, and suddenly there was nothing she could do to stop a massive sneeze.

"A-TISHOO!"

Greeny and Jack Frost whirled around and saw Rachel in the make-up box with the clef necklace.

"The necklace!" thundered Jack Frost.

"A pesky fairy!" squawked Greeny.

Before anyone else could move, Jack Frost sprang forward and slammed shut the lid of the make-up box.

"Gotcha!" he cackled. "Now I'm taking you home with me!"

Kirsty jumped to her feet.

"No!" she cried. "Bring her back!" But there was nothing she could do! Jack Frost held up his wand and disappeared in a flash of icy magic – together with the make-up box, the magical clef... *and Rachel*!

Greeny gave a squawk of rage. He tore off his tunic, stamped on it, and then charged out of the tent, yelling at the queue of children who were in his way.

Quickly, Frankie waved her wand.

Kirsty's pop-star look disappeared as she shrank down to fairy size.

"We have to rescue Rachel!" she said, fluttering her wings anxiously.

Frankie nodded. "We're going straight after her," she said.

She twirled her wand in the shape of a clef. Fairy dust swirled around them, lifting them into the air. They were on their way.

Inside the box, Rachel had no idea what had just happened. She could feel the box moving as it was carried along. Someone was cackling and muttering.

"I have to see what's going on,"
Rachel said to herself.

She pushed against the lid as hard as
she could. It was very heavy, but she
managed to open it a little way and
wedge it open with a make-up brush.
Now she could hear the voice clearly.
It was Jack Frost, and he sounded very
pleased with himself.

"I'll show those pesky fairies who's
really in charge around here," he said.
"No one can stop me now!"

Rachel peeped out through the small
opening and gave a gasp of horror.

She was in Fairyland. Jack Frost had
brought her to his Ice Castle!

The Glitter Trail

Rachel reached into a make-up pot and scooped out a handful of sparkling pink and purple glitter. Then she pushed it out through the narrow opening in the lid. She felt sure that Kirsty and Frankie would come to find her. When they did, perhaps they would have a glittery trail to follow!

Jack Frost carried the box through the kitchen and up a winding flight of stairs to his bedroom. Through the partly open lid, Rachel saw him gaze at his face in a large, gilt-edged mirror.

"I really am a handsome fellow," he said, stroking his chin. "And now, thanks to that silly fairy's clef, I'll be able to look even better!"

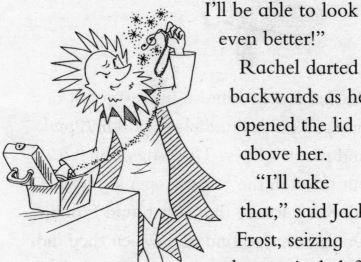

Rachel darted backwards as he opened the lid above her.

"I'll take that," said Jack Frost, seizing the magical clef necklace.

He placed it around his neck, and looked into the mirror.

"It's suits me very well, don't you agree?" he said.

Rachel decided to play along with him. After all, Frankie and Kirsty might already be in the castle, looking for her. She had to keep Jack Frost talking. "Oh yes," she said. "It makes you look very… er… magical."

"Pass me that brush," Jack Frost ordered. "And that pot of blue powder there. And the silver glitter. Quickly!"

Rachel did as she was told. She watched as Jack Frost began to paint a beautiful icy blue lightning flash across his face. Where were Frankie and Kirsty – and would they find her glitter trail in time?

Kirsty felt a chill on her arms and
legs, and then realised with delight
that she had filmy wings on her back.
With a swish of her wand, Frankie had
transported them both from Greeny's
make-up tent to the courtyard of Jack
Frost's Ice Castle.

Kirsty blinked the fairy
dust out of her eyes.
There was no sign
of Jack Frost
or of Rachel.
But her eagle
eyes noticed
something
shimmering
pink and
purple on the
cold flagstones.

"Look, Frankie – make-up!" she said.
"Let's follow it!"

They flew quickly, keeping their eyes
on the glittery trail. But when it led
them into the kitchen, they were dazzled!
The room was full of shiny metal bowls,
polished chrome handles, mirrored
cupboards and gleaming pots and pans.
The glittery trail was reflected back at
the fairies hundreds of thousands of times.

"I can't tell which is the real trail and which is a reflection!" cried Kirsty, rubbing her eyes.

"Keep your eyes on the ground," said Frankie. "Don't look up!"

They flew so close to the ground that their knees brushed against the floor tiles. But they found the real trail again, and followed it out of the kitchen and up to Jack Frost's bedroom. The door was open, and they peeped inside. Rachel was flitting around Jack Frost, handing him make-up brushes and powders. He was squinting into the mirror, painting icicles on his eyelids.

There seemed to be no way of getting
the clef back now that it was hanging
around his neck. But the reflections in
the kitchen had given Kirsty an idea.

"Have you
ever seen a
fairground
mirror?"
she asked
Frankie.
"Could
your magic
make Jack Frost

think that his make-up looks terrible?"

Frankie gave a cheeky grin and
nodded. Together, they flew into the
room and hid behind the mirror. Rachel
was hovering close by, and her face lit
up when she saw them.

"Rachel, can you get Jack Frost to close his eyes?" Kirsty whispered.

Rachel nodded and fluttered closer to Jack Frost, who was just finishing the last icicle.

"Those look wonderful," said Rachel. "Perhaps you should close your eyes to let them dry properly? It would be a shame to smudge them after all your hard work."

"You're right," said Jack Frost, closing his eyes at once. "My make-up has to be perfect!"

Frankie darted out from behind the mirror and swished her wand across the surface. It rippled like water on a pond, and then Frankie hid out of sight again.

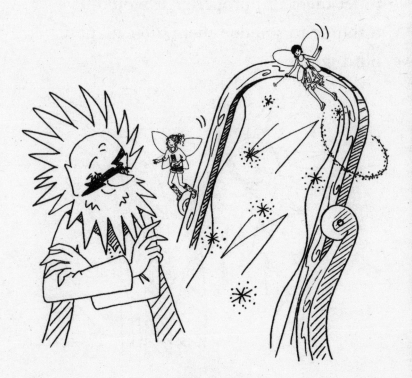

"You can open your eyes now," said Rachel.

Jack Frost opened his eyes and looked into the mirror...

Wibble-Wobble!

Jack Frost made a strange, croaking
noise in his throat.

"What – is – *that*?" he choked.

Frankie had transformed his mirror into
wibbly-wobbly fairground glass! Jack's
reflection showed a tiny head with an
enormous chin, all smeared in blue
and silver.

"I look ridiculous!" he screeched. "What's wrong with that stupid fairy necklace?"

"Perhaps the clef's magic works differently for you," said Rachel quickly. "Maybe you should let me have it back after all!"

"No chance!" bellowed Jack Frost. "It's MINE!"

He stomped around the bedroom in a fury, and Rachel darted behind the mirror. She hugged Kirsty and Frankie.

"Thank you for coming to rescue me!" she said. "But how are we going to get the magical clef back now?"

"Making him look terrible didn't work," said Kirsty thoughtfully. "I wonder what would happen if Frankie fixed the mirror?"

"It's worth a try," said Frankie, tapping the mirror with her wand.

Rachel fluttered up and perched on top of the mirror frame. Jack Frost was still stamping around, kicking pieces of furniture and scowling.

"Why don't you take another look?" Rachel suggested. "Maybe it's not as bad as you think."

"Don't be stupid!" roared Jack Frost. But as he glared at her, he caught a glimpse of himself in the mirror. This time, the reflection was perfect. Jack Frost's mouth fell open. Thanks to the magical clef necklace, he had never looked so good!

Enchanted by his own face, Jack Frost

moved closer to the mirror. He couldn't take his eyes off his own reflection.

Slowly, Frankie and Kirsty slipped out from behind the mirror.

They fluttered behind Jack Frost and
carefully unhooked the necklace. Staring
dreamily at his reflection, Jack Frost
didn't notice a thing as they pulled the
magical clef from
his neck.

As soon
as it was in
Frankie's
hands, it shrank
to fairy size.

"So handsome…" murmured Jack
Frost, turning his face so he could see
both sides.

"Let's get back to Rainspell Island!"
whispered Frankie.

With a wave of her wand, the three
friends disappeared, leaving Jack Frost
alone… but very happy!

On Rainspell Island that evening, fans were in for a treat. Dakota May was about to give her surprise performance, and Rachel and Kirsty were standing in the front row.

"Thank goodness make-up is back to normal," said Rachel. "We can really relax and celebrate now."

She had a brightly coloured rainbow painted on her cheek and Kirsty's face was sparkling with fairy glitter. The designs had been conjured up by Frankie, who was hidden beneath Kirsty's hair so that she could enjoy the concert too.

"But Jack Frost still has two of the clefs," said Kirsty with a sigh. "There are still two more Pop Star Fairies who need our help. I hope this concert will go all right while those two necklaces are missing."

"My clef will provide just enough magic for this performance to turn out perfectly," said Frankie. "I know you'll help Rochelle and Una just like you've helped me... but right now it's time to dance!"

The crowd went crazy as Dakota May bounced on to the stage. She looked completely different from earlier. She had her familiar shiny black bob instead of the long blonde wig, and her perfect make-up made her glow. But what really lit up the stage was her big, beaming smile.

"Welcome to Rainspell Island, everyone!" she said. "This is a place that's all about friendship and helping each other. I'd like to dedicate the next song to two girls who helped me today. They know who they are!"

Frankie, Kirsty and Rachel cheered as the music started and Dakota's clear, beautiful voice soared out across the cheering crowd. It was the girls' favourite song – *The Faces of Me*.

"It might seem that I have different faces,
For different people and different places.
But in my heart I'm still me,
That's who I will always be."

Kirsty and Rachel shared a happy smile. Pop music was still in danger and they were facing perilous adventures. But just for this evening they were going to dance and enjoy the music – just like everyone else!

**Now Kirsty and Rachel
must help...**

Rochelle the Star Spotter Fairy

Read on for a sneak peek...

"Another gorgeous morning at the
Rainspell Island Music Festival!" said
Kirsty Tate happily. "Do you think
I should wear this daisy headband,
Rachel?"

Her best friend Rachel Walker looked
at their reflections in the shower block
mirror.

"Definitely!" she said with a smile.
"The white petals look pretty against
your dark hair."

The girls had just finished showering
and getting dressed. They were camping

at the festival with Rachel's parents, and they were all special guests of The Angels pop group.

"I think you should wear my rose headband," Kirsty said, handing it to Rachel. "It will really suit you."

"I feel so lucky to be here," said Rachel as she arranged the headband in her hair. "I've lost count of all the amazing things we've done – and the fabulous concerts we've been to!"

"As well as the fun we've had helping the fairies," said Kirsty with a twinkle in her eyes.

No one knew that the girls were friends with the people of Fairyland. They had often helped the fairies to outwit bad-tempered Jack Frost and his mischievous goblins. Soon after they arrived on Rainspell Island, they had met the Pop Star Fairies, who used their magical clef necklaces to look after pop music. Jack Frost and his goblins had stolen the clefs and brought them to the festival to help Jack become a pop star. So far, Kirsty and Rachel had helped five of the Pop Star Fairies to find their magic clefs.

"I just hope that we can find the two missing clefs before the end of the festival," said Rachel.

"Me too," said Kirsty. "It would be terrible if Jack Frost managed to ruin it for everyone. There are still lots of fantastic concerts to look forward to."

"Yes, I can't wait to see Jacob Bright at the Talent of Tomorrow show later," said Rachel. "He's one of the biggest up-and-coming stars here."

"And we still haven't seen Jax Tempo perform," said Kirsty. "I wonder when he'll be on stage. He must be very good to get so famous so quickly – I hadn't even heard of him until the start of the festival."

"Well, I'm ready," said Rachel. "Let's get our things and go back to the tent."

Kirsty put her hairbrush and spare hairbands back into her sponge bag, while Rachel went into the shower cubicle to get her shampoo. But as she leaned over the shower tray, she noticed that the remaining bubbles were sparkling with rainbow colours.

Rachel felt a prickle of excitement running up and down her spine...

Read Rochelle the Star Spotter Fairy to find out what adventures are in store for Kirsty and Rachel!

Meet the
Pop Star Fairies

Kirsty and Rachel have to save Rainspell Island Music Festival after Jack Frost steals the Pop Star Fairies' musical clef necklaces!

www.rainbowmagicbooks.co.uk

Meet the fairies, play games
and get sneak peeks at
the latest books!

www.rainbowmagicbooks.co.uk

There's fairy fun for everyone on
our wonderful website.
You'll find great activities, competitions, stories and
fairy profiles, and also a special newsletter.

Get 30% off all Rainbow Magic books at

www.rainbowmagicbooks.co.uk

Enter the code RAINBOW at the checkout.
Offer ends 31 December 2013.

Offer valid in United Kingdom and Republic of Ireland only.

Look out for the next sparkly
Rainbow Magic Special!

Robyn the Christmas Party Fairy

Rachel and Kirsty are helping to organise a big Christmas party.
But Jack Frost has stolen Robyn the Christmas Party Fairy's
magical objects! The girls must help Robyn,
before the spirit of Christmas is lost forever...

Out now!

Alexandra
the Royal Baby
Fairy

Out in
May 2013

 Also available
as an ebook

The whole of Fairyland is very excited - there's going
to be a new royal baby! But when the special baby
goes missing, Rachel and Kirsty are there to help
their friend, Alexandra the Royal Baby Fairy.

www.rainbowmagicbooks.co.uk

Meet the
Princess Fairies

Jack Frost has stolen the Princess Fairies' tiaras. Kirsty and Rachel must get them back before all the magic in the world fades away!

www.rainbowmagicbooks.co.uk